RAIN

PREQUEL

THE MARS DIARIES

SKYE MACKINNON

Peryton Press

Copyright © 2018 by Skye MacKinnon

All rights reserved.

No part of this book may be reproduced in any form or by any electronic
or mechanical means, including information storage and retrieval
systems, without written permission from the author, except for the use
of brief quotations in a book review.

Cover by Peryton Covers

Published by Peryton Press

perytonpress.com

CONTENTS

CHAPTER 1

The world's end wasn't full of screaming and explosions. No, it was a weather report. A stupid, boring weather report. Most people never even realised what had happened, until it was too late. Not that anyone could have prevented the Drowning. Not recently, anyway. Climate change had been happening for decades and this was the day nature struck back.

Rain. Lots of rain. It's raining now and it's been raining for five days. Non-stop. In the entire country. Most of the world. Even Africa has rain storms like they've not experienced since records began.

Cellars are flooding, bridges have closed, entire villages are having to be evacuated as rivers break from their beds and swallow the dwellings built too close to their banks. And still, it's raining.

I shake my head and turn back to my computer. It's no use dwelling on what's happened. I need to focus on what's happening now, and on our future. The people deciding our future, the future of the human race.

I check the systems on the station. Everything seems to be normal. No abnormal readings. Good, that means this might actually be a relaxing day. There's enough chaos on Earth, I don't need chaos on Mars as well.

A calendar reminder pops up on my screen. Five minutes until I'm to contact the colonists for their daily update. Mostly, it's a formality. We can check on their life support systems from here, so they don't need to tell us. Their psychologist and doctor send us weekly reports and so does the senior engineer. Still, it's important for them to have a link to Earth. With the recent solar activity, the colonists have missed out on a lot of calls home. I might not be a relative, but I think I've become something of a friend to Pete and Suzie, the two people responsible for keeping in touch with me. I never met either of them in person; I hadn't started this job yet when they left Earth. Some days though, I feel like I've known them for ages and have had proper conversations with them, not just quick written messages that are kept as short as possible to deal with the time delay between Mars and Earth.

I get myself a cup of tea from the dispenser and like every day, I vow to bring a proper kettle to the office. The water is never quite hot enough for tea, especially not after adding milk.

I sit back and wait for the first message from Mars to arrive.

SUZIE

Hey control. How's it going?

CONTROL

It's raining. You guys are lucky you don't have rain up there.

SUZIE

I'm sure our greenhouses would be grateful for some rain. We lost another batch of veggies because we didn't have enough water.

I make a quick note of that. I'll need to have to add that to the report later on, or at least check if someone else has mentioned it in their notes. Everything happening on Mars has to be properly documented. Nothing is routine, everything is new and exciting. We're recording the progress of the colonists for future missions, future generations even.

CONTROL

You can have some of the water currently flooding my basement. Anyway, how is everyone?

SUZIE

Laura is ill, but the Doc thinks it's just a hefty cold. He'll put it in his report.

CONTROL

Hope she gets better soon.

SUZIE

So do I. She's the best cook ever. Xi-Yang was making lunch today and it was horrible.

CONTROL

Anything else to report?

I sip on my tea while waiting for an answer. Definitely not hot enough. I dunk a biscuit in it for good measure. Suzie is taking her sweet time. Maybe there are chores she doesn't want to get back to straight away. It wouldn't be the first time she's prolonged our conversations to have some quiet from the chaos of life on the Mars station.

After two biscuits, I get impatient.

CONTROL

Suzie?

SUZIE

Sorry, Doc was here. Laura has started vomiting. Bad cramps as well. And Mac is complaining of a headache too. I better get back to work and help Doc look after Laura.

CONTROL

Okay, let me know if it gets worse.

I sit back and stare at the screen. Our colonists rarely get ill. They've all been chosen for their physical robustness and they get a large dose of supplements every morning to make sure that they get all the nutrients they need. While they've managed to grow quite a few varieties of fruit and vegetables on the station, they don't have a sustainable source of protein.

Of course, the only ways to get sick on Mars is from existing germs that have come there with the settlers. There's no life on Mars, at least none that we've identified so far.

"Lacey, everything alright?"

Joan, my supervisor, leans over the edge of my cubicle and smiles at me. She's probably the nicest boss I've ever had, yet I know that it can't have just been nicety that got her where she is now. There's a strength behind her pretty face that doesn't always show.

"Two colonists have fallen ill. They're going to keep us updated."

She looks surprised but doesn't comment on it.

"Your wife called," she says. "She needs help getting all your possessions onto the first floor. The flooding is about to spill from the basement onto the ground floor."

My heart sinks. All our books are in the living room.

Joan gives me an understanding smile. "I'm giving you the rest of the day off. Go home and make sure you don't lose anything important."

I want to hug her, but I manage to refrain from doing so. Instead, I quickly pack up my things and debate what route to take home. It's still raining.

It's taken hours to carry everything up the stairs, but I'm glad we did it. Three inches of water are now covering the floor.

Luckily, the roof is still holding, not like that of our neighbours who now have water coming in from above and below.

I switch on the tv to watch the weather report. Fingers crossed the rain is going to end soon. The news are still on and I check my watch. It should be the weather report by now. I turn up the volume to hear what's going on.

"The latest data shows that there has been a massive release of greenhouse gasses in the Russian tundra, caused by the ongoing rain thawing the permafrost..."

"Kate!" I call to my wife. "Have you seen this?"

She comes into the living room and sits down next to me on the sofa.

"What's up?"

I point at the telly. "Greenhouse gasses have been released."

"So?"

I sigh. "This is big. They've been trapped by the permafrost for millions of years and now the rain has set them free. Climate change won't be unstoppable now."

"Should we pack our bags and move to Mars?" She's smiling but I know her well enough to recognise the tiny worry wrinkles around her eyes.

"They'd never take me," I sigh. "They won't take people who're diabetic."

"It was a joke, sweetie." She puts an arm around my shoulders and pulls me close. "So, this is really bad?"

She doesn't know much about science. She's an artist at heart and even though she's a receptionist by day, she spends most evenings in her little studio in the attic. One day, I'm hoping I'll earn enough for her to be able to be a full-time artist, but for now, the studio is all we can afford. ESA doesn't pay as much as NASA does.

"Yes, it's bad. This was supposed to happen over decades or longer, not all in one go. Maybe they got the readings wrong. Maybe it's a mistake..."

I let my voice trail off, but there's no deceiving either myself or my wife. This is a catastrophe.

I hug her and concentrate on her warmth and soft-ness. I don't want to think of the end of the world just now. Sometimes, knowledge can be a burden. But would I rather be ignorant and walk towards our planet's death like a pig to the slaughterhouse?

CHAPTER 2

The mood in the office is grim. Everyone's seen the news and many of our scientists are involved in validating the data just now. There are scenarios that were drawn up for something like this happening, but not so soon, not so quickly.

My calendar alert pops up like every day. We've decided not to tell the colonists for now. We don't want them to worry about their friends and families on Earth. They need to concentrate on their own survival on Mars.

I log on and sip on my tea. It's a day like any other and yet it feels like we've stumbled into a new world overnight.

CONTROL

Hello?

SUZIE

Morning. We have a problem.

My heart drops. Not another one.

SUZIE

Laura is really sick. She's vomiting up blood and she's in a lot of pain. Doc doesn't know what's wrong. He wants to talk to experts on Earth.

CONTROL

I'll set something up. What about Mac?

SUZIE

Headache and cramps. No vomit yet but it looks like he might have the same illness. We've not had anything like this before. People are worried.

CONTROL

I'll inform people here, we'll put together a team. Even if they'll get better, it's a good training situation. I should have some people here in an hour. Does that work for Doc?

SUZIE

Yes, the sooner, the better.

CONTROL

Don't worry, we'll deal with this. How are you feeling?

SUZIE

...

CONTROL

Suzie?

SUZIE

I have a headache. Maybe it's just stress.

I swallow hard. This is getting worse and worse.

CONTROL

I'll set up a meeting. See you in an hour!

As soon as she's disconnected, I get up and hurry to my supervisor's desk. Joan is busy typing but looks up as soon as I clear my throat.

"Yes?"

"Mac's vomiting blood," I say without preamble. "Their doctor wants to talk to some experts down here."

Her usual smile disappears and she turns serious. "Let me make some calls. Is it just Laura?"

"Mac is showing symptoms too. Suzie has a headache, but let's hope that's not a sign of whatever the other two have."

She nods grimly. "I'll get on it. I think we'll need a video conference for this. Can you set everything up and pull up the sick colonists' files? I'm not sure all the experts I have on call will be familiar with each of them."

"Of course."

Adrenaline is spreading through me as I hastily get everything organised. We have monthly video calls, but they all follow a set protocol. This is different.

I don't like change, especially not if it comes with danger attached to it.

By the time I've set up everything, we have five experts on the line. Two virologists, one woman specialising in space medicine and two doctors who I'm sure are authorities in their fields as well. Joan and I are sitting in the meeting room in front of a giant screen, waiting for the Mars colony to dial in. We've briefed the experts and they're busy reading the files about Laura and Mac. I've pulled up Suzie's file as well, just in case.

A message pops up on the screen. A video recording. I was expecting to be communicating with them via text message like we usually do because it's a lot quicker. Videos take a lot of time to download, and even longer to upload and send to Mars.

PETE

Hey Earthlings

I smile when his transmission appears on my laptop. He's not lost his sense of humour yet.

CONTROL

We got your video, just waiting for it to download. What's the situation?

PETE

Suzie's had to lie down, she's not feeling well. Two others are complaining of headaches. Doc will be here in a moment, but better watch the video first.

"That sounds ominous," Joan observes. I agree. What's in the video?

After two anxious minutes, the download is finally complete and the video player opens. Doc – his real name is James but nobody uses that – is looking at the camera, his expression grave.

"I don't know how much you've been told, so here's a quick summary. We have two people ill and another three showing first symptoms. It starts with a headache, followed by vomiting and cramps, then coughing up blood. I've given them all the standard meds to deal with their symptoms, but they're not showing any effect at all, not even painkillers."

The camera swerves and shows us a view of the Martian hospital room. There are three beds, two of which are occupied by Laura and Mac. Both of them have a host of sensors attached to them. An empty blood bag hangs above Laura's bed, but she looks incredibly pale, despite the transfusion.

"Laura's deteriorating fast," Doc continues, his voice a little quieter now as if he doesn't want his patients to hear. "She's slowly losing consciousness and there's nothing I seem to be able to do about it."

He points at Mac, who weakly waves to the camera. "Mac's vomited, but there's no blood as of yet. I'm hoping it's a lighter form of whatever Laura has, or maybe something different altogether."

Doc turns the camera again until it's focussed on him. "To be honest, I have no idea what this is. It's progressing fast and none of the drugs I have show an effect. I've taken blood samples, but there's nothing out of the ordinary, although of course, I don't have any sophisticated testing methods here. I'll be sending all the readings in a moment. I'd be grateful for some advice."

He looks frustrated and worried. Not a good sign.

"I've just received the measurements he mentioned," Joan tells the experts. "Forwarding them to you now."

While they look at whatever the readings show, I write a quick message to Mars.

CONTROL

Watched the video. Experts are looking at the samples now. Is Doc there yet?

PETE

Yes, he's sitting next to me and is ready to answer any questions they may have

Joan and I exchange a glance while we wait for the five experts to say something. This isn't good. Laura looked really ill and I'm worried about her. I've never met her, but from what I've heard, she sounds nice.

"I recommend a quarantine," one of the virologists suddenly declares. "It's spreading far too quickly and until we find a cure, it's imperative to keep the affected separate from the healthy."

"I agree," Professor Mischler, a doctor, says. "As long as we don't know what we're dealing with, let's be as cautious as possible."

CONTROL

They suggest a quarantine.

PETE

Doc agrees, he was about to propose that too. But he asks who should be quarantined? We all interact with each other all day, so if we want to quarantine everyone who's been in contact with Laura in the past two days, that would be at least half of all colonists.

I pose the question to the experts. Nobody says anything for a while.

"As many as possible," the second virologist finally replies. "I know it's not feasible to have a proper quarantine there like we would here on Earth, but maybe they can restrict the time people spend in community areas? As little physical contact as possible."

I relay his answer to Pete and Doc.

PETE

Doc says he'll ask everyone who presents symptoms to stay in the hospital area for now.

"I'm sorry, I have to leave," the space medicine expert suddenly says, interrupted by a loud siren that must be in her building. "I think there's a fire somewhere."

"That's not a fire alarm," Joan winces. "It's a tsunami alert."

"A tsunami? In Ireland?" The woman's voice has turned panicked. "That must be a mist-"

Her video feed cuts out and we're left staring at a black screen.

Joan clears her throat. "Let's reconvene later when

we know what's going on. Lacey will keep you informed of any further messages we get from Mars."

I nod, already pulling up Twitter on my phone. There really is a tsunami racing towards Ireland's West coast.

"Do you think this is a hoax?" I ask Joan who's also staring at her phone.

"I'm afraid it's not. There's another tsunami warning in Japan and another in Thailand. Something is happening to this planet." She sighs. "Let's not tell Mars, they've got enough to deal with as it is."

"Even those who have family in those countries?"

Joan nods decisively. "Yes. Don't tell them anything for now."

CHAPTER 3

Overnight, the media have coined the term The Drowning for the weather events currently affecting the entire world. Never-ending rain, tsunamis, thunderstorms, earthquakes. It's as if the planet has suddenly decided to rid itself of all life on its surface.

Only half the usual staff are in the office. The rest of us is dazed and shocked. Thousands of people died yesterday and millions are missing. How many more will die today?

It's almost a relief to be able to focus on Mars's problems. As big as they seem to the colonists, as small they are to me when compared to the death and destruction facing Earth.

PETE

Bad news.

Okay, maybe their problems aren't small. I take a

deep breath, hoping that the worst case scenario hasn't happened.

CONTROL

What is it?

PETE

Laura died early this morning. Mac has started coughing blood. Doc isn't looking good either, he's thrown up twice but he's refusing to lie down.

CONTROL

I'm so sorry! What about Suzie?

PETE

Vomiting. As are seven others.

I stare at my screen. This must be a nightmare. Death on Mars, death on Earth, all at the same time.

CONTROL

You?

PETE

Headache. But I think most of us are having a headache by now.

CONTROL

Our experts haven't been able to find anything conclusive in the data Doc sent. They recommend staying hydrated and treating the symptoms.

PETE

I'll pass it on to Doc, but that's what he's been doing anyway. We've stopped doing all but the most essential tasks around the station so we can care for those who're ill. And most of us have recorded videos we'd like you to send to our families.

I take a deep breath. Videos for their families. That sounds like they're starting to give up already. So far, we've kept the illness of the colonists a secret. Not even their next of kin know. Not that the media would care at the moment. A month ago, it would have been big news, but now, people are focussed on Earth rather than on what happens on Mars.

CONTROL

I'll forward them. Anything else I can do for you?

PETE

Think of us. Pray for us, if you're religious. And hope that we'll get through this. Somehow.

EPILOGUE

Two days without any news from Mars. I've got an automated message set up that pings them every hour, but I've not had a reply so far. I wonder if they're all dead.It's a terrible thought but I've always been a realist.

Now though, I wish I wasn't. My wife's parents died yesterday and there's no time to mourn them. There are friends and family dying everywhere. The hospitals can't cope, neither can the morgues.

Instead of dealing with it all, I'm in the office, one of the few people who are here. My screen is blank, there are no emails in my inbox except for notices about who's died.

A ping makes me look up. One of my previous messages has been answered.

CONTROL

Is anyone there?

LOUISE

Hi, this is Louise. I'm a geologist and I'm the last person alive.

CONTROL

Are you sick as well?

LOUISE

Not anymore. But I'm alone. The last human on Mars.

If you have not read **The Mars Diaries** *yet, start with* **Alone** *or get all three parts in the box set.*

Continue flicking the page for a list of all my sci-fi romance books.

Keep up to date with my latest releases and get a FREE eBook by signing up to my newsletter: skyemackinnon. com/newsletter

Buy your books direct from the author

GET 20% OFF YOUR NEXT EBOOK OR AUDIOBOOK!

USE CODE BOOKWORMS AT
SKYEMACKINNON.COM/SHOP

Happy reading!

Find all of Skye's books on her website, **skyemackinnon.com**, where you can also order signed paperbacks and swag.

Many of her books are available as audiobooks.

SCIENCE FICTION ROMANCE

Set in the Starlight Universe

- **Starlight Vikings** (sci-fi m/f romance)
- **Starlight Monsters** (sci-fi m/f romance)
- **Starlight Highlanders Mail Order Brides** (sci-fi m/f romance, part of the Intergalactic Dating Agency)
- **The Intergalactic Guide to Humans** (sci-fi romance with various pairings)
- **Starlight Mermen** (sci-fi m/f romance)

Set in other worlds

- **Between Rebels** (sci-fi reverse harem set in the Planet Athion shared world)
- **The Mars Diaries** (sci-fi reverse harem)
- **Aliens and Animals** (f/f sci-fi romance co-written with Arizona Tape)

PARANORMAL & FANTASY ROMANCE

- **Claiming Her Bears** (post-apocalyptic shifter reverse harem)
- **Daughter of Winter** (fantasy reverse harem)
- **Catnip Assassins** (urban fantasy reverse harem)
- **Infernal Descent** (paranormal reverse harem based on Dante's Inferno, co-written with Bea Paige)
- **Seven Wardens** (fantasy reverse harem co-written with Laura Greenwood)
- **The Lost Siren** (post-apocalyptic, paranormal reverse harem co-written with Liza Street)

OTHER SERIES

- **Academy of Time** (time travel academy standalones, reverse harem and m/f)
- **Defiance** (contemporary reverse harem with a hint of thriller/suspense)

STANDALONES

- Song of Souls – m/f fantasy romance, fairy tale retelling
- Their Hybrid – steampunk reverse harem
- Partridge in the P.E.A.R. - sci-fi reverse harem co-written with Arizona Tape
- Highland Butterflies – sapphic romance
- Wings of Time and Fate - epic fantasy

ANTHOLOGIES AND BOX SETS

- Hungry for More – charity cookbook
- Daggers & Destiny – a fantasy romance starter library
- Stars & Seduction - a science fiction romance starter library

ABOUT THE AUTHOR

Skye MacKinnon is a Scottish romance author who was raised by elves in the mystical Highlands and calls the Loch Ness monster her friend. Her bestselling books weave together romance with action, suspense and whimsical humour, creating page-turners filled with strong heroines, alpha heroes and loveable monsters.

Whether she's writing about aliens in kilts, hunky Vikings or cat shifter assassins, Skye likes to put a new spin on familiar tropes. Some of her heroines don't have to choose, some fall in love with other women, and others get abducted by clueless aliens.

Skye lives with her bossy cat on the west coast of Scotland and uses the dramatic views from her office as an inspiration, no matter whether she writes fantasy, paranormal or science fiction romance. Until she gets abducted by aliens, that is.

Subscribe to her newsletter:
skyemackinnon.com/newsletter

Printed in Great Britain
by Amazon

48073756R00020